Daddy and Tom

GO SHOPPING

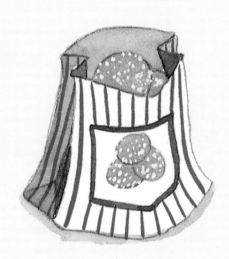

Illustrations by

Louise Comfort

DEAN

One Saturday morning, Tom and his Daddy go to the supermarket. Daddy gives Tom the shopping list to hold.

"We've got to get everything on this list,"
says Daddy. "Apples and bananas, soap,
cheese, orange juice and bread. Then,
if you're good, I'll buy you a treat!"

"The first thing on the list is apples," says Daddy. "Help me to put these in the scales, Tom."

"Now we need bananas,"
says Daddy. "Can you see them, Tom?"
Tom points to the bananas.

"Let's see," says Daddy, putting the bananas into the trolley. "Apples, bananas . . . soap!"

He takes a packet
off the shelf. Tom reaches
out for a red washing-up brush.

"That's not
on the list," says
Daddy. "I don't think
Mummy would be very pleased
if we came home with that!"

Apples, bananas, soap . . . cheese is the next thing on the list.

Kate and her daddy need cheese too.
The shop assistant has given her some to try.

"I want some!" says Tom.
The shop assistant cuts a small
piece for Tom.

"What do you think of that?"
asks Daddy.
"Yuck!" says Tom,
screwing up
his face.

"Let's see," says Daddy, "we've got apples, bananas, soap, cheese . . ."
Tom thinks they need some jam, too.
He reaches out
for a jar.

"Watch out!" cries Daddy.
He catches the jar just in time.
"That was close! I'll take the things off
the shelves. Where's the orange juice?"

Tom and Daddy like the bakery best because it smells so good.
"Bread!" says Tom, pointing.

Daddy chooses a loaf and some doughnuts. Tom leans over to dip his hand in the sugary bag.

"You deserve a treat for being good," says Daddy. "But wait until we get home!"

Now it's time to pay.

Tom helps to pack the shopping bags.
In go all the things on the shopping list.

Apples, bananas, soap, cheese, orange juice,
bread . . . and doughnuts!

"You've been a great help, Tom," smiles Daddy.
"Now it's time for your treat."

Tom's New Potty

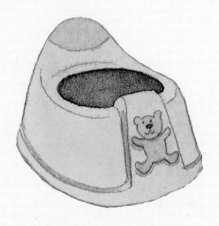

Illustrations by

Louise Comfort

DEAN

One day, Tom's Mummy brings home
a surprise.

"It's a potty!" says Mummy. "You can
sit on this instead of wearing
your nappy."

"But I'm happy in my nappy," says Tom.

Tom hides the potty where Mummy can't find it.

"Where did you put the potty, Tom?" asks Mummy.

Perhaps the potty will stay lost forever!

Tom is racing his cars on the carpet.
"Look what I've found!" says Mummy.

"Why don't you give the potty a try now?"
"No, Mummy," says Tom. "I like my nappy!"

"Vroom, vroom, VROOOM!"
Suddenly, the yellow car shoots under the sofa.
"I'll use the potty!" says Tom.

The potty speeds across the floor.
Mummy puts her head into the room.
"Have you tried your potty yet, Tom?"
"No, " says Tom. "I'm happy in my nappy!"

Tom won't sit on the potty! Ever!

But it might be good for other things.

It's a mixing bowl for a cook . . .

. . . or a seat for Teddy . . .

. . . or how about a crown? I'm Prince Potty!

Tom goes to Sue's house during the day. "I thought we'd play in the garden today," says Sue. "Tom, you can bring your potty."

Prince Potty is driving the royal car!

He keeps the royal treasure
safe in the potty crown.

Prince Potty goes digging in the sandpit next. The crown makes a good bucket too!

Then all at once, he stops digging. His nappy is wet, and he feels uncomfortable.

Then he has an **idea**.

He tips out the sand, wriggles out of his nappy . . .

. . . and sits down on the potty.

Tom's Mummy arrives at the end of the day.
"Well done!" she says, and gives him a hug.